I am an ARO PUBLISHING
TEN WORD BOOK:

My ten words are:

night	scratch
listen	monster
drip	no
tick	there
squeak	are

Night Monsters

10 WORDS

Story by SHARON SIGMOND SHEBAR
Pictures by BOB REESE

Night, night.

Listen.

Drip

Drip

Drip

Drip

Tick

Tick

Tick

Tick

Squeak

Squeak

Squeak

Squeak

Scratch

Scratch

Scratch

Scratch

Monsters!

Night monsters!

Drip
Drip
Drip
Drip

Drip

Drip

Drip

Drip

No monster.

Tick

Tick

Tick

Tick

Tick

Tick

Tick

Tick

No
monster.

Squeak
Squeak
Squeak
Squeak

Squeak
Squeak
Squeak
Squeak

No monster.

Scratch
Scratch

Scratch

Scratch

There are no

night monsters.